Suite
for
Human Nature

For Anselme
—E. P.

ATHENEUM BOOKS FOR YOUNG READERS
An imprint of Simon & Schuster Children's Publishing Division
1230 Avenue of the Americas, New York, New York 10020
Text copyright © 2016 by Diane Charlotte Lampert
Illustrations copyright © 2016 by Eric Puybaret
All rights reserved, including the right of reproduction in whole or in part in any form.
ATHENEUM BOOKS FOR YOUNG READERS is a registered trademark of Simon & Schuster, Inc.
Atheneum logo is a trademark of Simon & Schuster, Inc.
For information about special discounts for bulk purchases, please contact Simon & Schuster Special Sales at 1-866-506-1949 or business@simonandschuster.com.
The Simon & Schuster Speakers Bureau can bring authors to your live event. For more information or to book an event, contact the Simon & Schuster Speakers Bureau at 1-866-248-3049 or visit our website at www.simonspeakers.com.
Book design by Debra Sfetsios-Conover
The text for this book is set in Goldenbook.
The illustrations for this book are rendered in acrylic on linen.
Manufactured in China
0216 SCP
First Edition
10 9 8 7 6 5 4 3 2 1
CIP data for this book is available from the Library of Congress
ISBN 978-1-4169-5373-9
ISBN 978-1-4814-6357-7 (eBook)

Suite
for
Human Nature

by Diane Charlotte Lampert

Illustrated by Eric Puybaret

Based on a musical composition
by Diane Charlotte Lampert and Wynton Marsalis

A Caitlyn Dlouhy Book

atheneum ATHENEUM BOOKS FOR YOUNG READERS

New York   London   Toronto   Sydney   New Delhi

ONCE UPON A MOUNTAIN there lived a young lady named Mother Nature. She was a very busy lady, for she had to care for everything that walked, flew, swam, crawled, and grew all over the Earth.

There was one kind of creature she cared for
most of all, because they needed all the help
they could get. They could not fly nor swim
nor roar nor gallop. Mother Nature felt very
sorry for them, so she let them live
in a warm, green garden and gave them
all they needed to eat and drink. In return,
she asked only that they help her take care of
things as best they could.

She named these creatures Humans.

Despite all that she had to look after, she longed for her own child. "One

to be my very own," she said with a sigh. So she took four sticks and two

pumpkin seeds and made her very first child.

Mother Nature was so happy that she named him Fear, as

it rhymed so well with "dear."

She was so happy that she barely noticed

how her child wobbled and shivered and was

always running from his own shadow

into his mother's arms.

She was so happy, she almost

forgot about mothering the Earth.

She had ponds to freeze, rabbits

to paint, and more snowflakes to

make than all the fingers and toes

in the world could count.

So she asked the Humans in her warm garden to watch Fear, and she dashed off to create winter.

All winter long, Fear played with the Humans. All winter long, his mother made snowflakes—no two alike—and turned noses red and cheeks rosy.

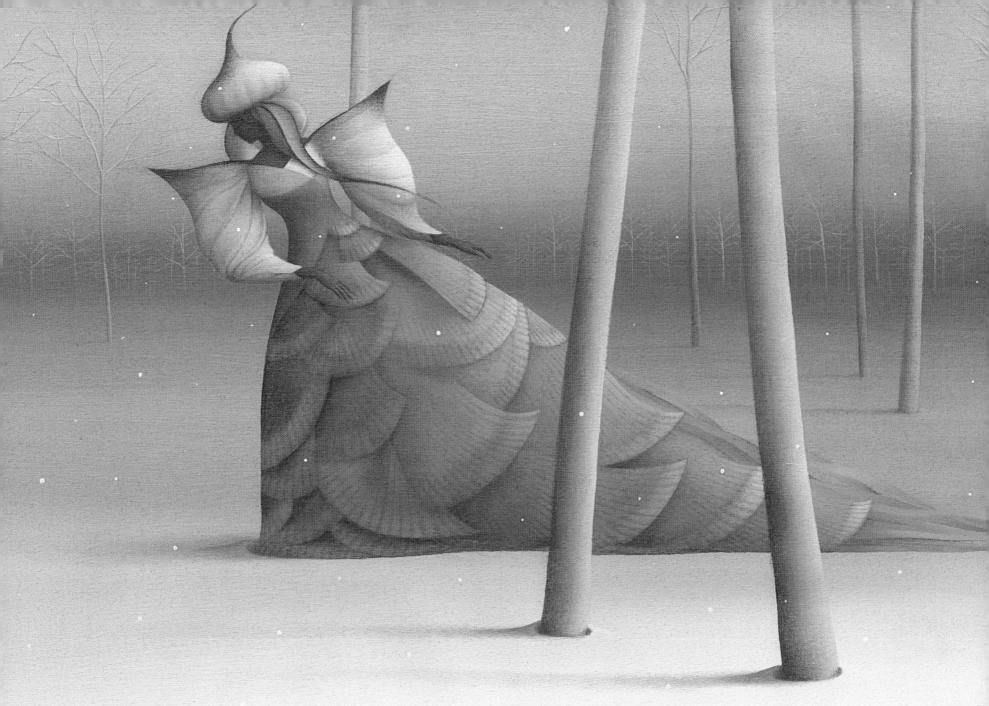

And when she finished melting the last snowman, she came home to a surprise, and not the good kind. Mice were afraid of cats, lambs ran away from lions, and little fish hid themselves from big fish. Worst of all, the Humans were just as fearful of one another as the child had been.

Oh, *this is not good*, she thought. But she knew first attempts at anything seldom succeeded.

She would try again! So she took four sticks and two stones and made her second child, Envy.

She set Envy down beside his brother, Fear, hoping the two would play together. But he paid Fear no attention, except when his mother played with Fear. That's when he wanted his brother to play with him. He fretted over who had more milk in their cups, who had the softer blanket. He even envied the mice running from the cats; they had tails and he had none.

But Mother Nature did not notice. Spring was on her mind, and she was at her busiest: waking up bulbs, warming winds, shaking the sand from dreams, and teaching ten billion birds to sing again.

So she left both children in the warm garden, cautioning the Humans not to let Envy play with any of the animals, for she had seen how they had caught fear from Fear.

The Humans did just what Mother Nature told them to do. They kept a careful eye on Envy, and they watched him fuss because birds got to have bright-colored feathers and his brother got to be older than him. Soon all of the Humans were grumbling over the fact they only had hair and couldn't fly, and by the way, antelopes have four legs and outrun them.

Stretching her legs, and between seasons,

Mother Nature returned home to concentrate on her boys.

Raising flowers was easy compared to raising these children. Maybe

a new child would come out different. "I'm thinking too small," Mother Nature

decided. So this time she took boulders and tree trunks and a glacier, and made her

third child. She named him Hate, to rhyme with "playmate," which is what she

hoped he would be to his two brothers.

Well. Hate shouted them down! Drowned them in growls!

Roared like a volcano! Muttered like thunder! Stomped and shook

the whole Earth with his great thumpy feet!

Little Fear feared Hate's hate, and Hate hated
Fear for fearing him.

Envy envied Hate's hate, while Hate, hating Envy, envied Envy's envy, and . . . to make matters worse, summertime was coming. Mother Nature had to ripen the fields, spruce the trees, and honey-up the bees.

She had to leave Hate and his brothers with the Humans. "This is a wild one," she warned them, so the Humans stayed very close to Hate, never letting him out of their sight. Tempers flared into tantrums. Playing became fighting. Brother no longer talked to brother.

When Mother Nature returned, she fretted. These children of hers weren't what she'd expected. Frustrated, she shook the leaves from the trees, sat in the middle of the pile, counted to ten, and dreamed up her fourth child.

This boy grew so quickly, she named him Greed, to rhyme with "weed."

Greed was soon big enough to grab his brothers' toys right out of their hands. He grabbed their food right out of their mouths. He grabbed everything in sight, especially anything that wasn't his.

And Envy was jealous of everything Greed grabbed.

Mother Nature knew she had to do
something about her wild boys. And she
would, just as soon as she got back from
creating autumn.

She brought her boys to the garden once
again and hurried off to make her yearly
one-woman show of red, yellow, and gold.

But when she returned, no one was reveling in the beauty she had created.

Her boys were snatching leaves from one another, draining the color out

of them. Greed, who grew bigger than Hate, had the biggest pile, and

now even the Humans were angry.

Needless to say, her children were interfering with everything.

Mother Nature could no longer handle her boys, their mischief,

and the world all at the same time.

Then it suddenly dawned on her: She couldn't run a world with just boys! "A sister! That's what they need." So she gathered the tenderest twigs, the flounciest feathers, and the gloss of a gossamer moth. And poof! There was a little girl among them. Mother Nature named her Fickle, as it was a fun word to say.

Living up to her name, Fickle was a spirited little girl, and her brothers lined up to play with her. But she couldn't make up her mind and flitted from brother to brother, delighting then leaving each one to flare up in his own particular way as she played with the next.

Winter came and went, and with spring in the air
Mother Nature was exhausted trying to
keep track of her daughter's off-and-on
desires. She handed her over to the
Humans. It was love at first sight.

Fickle sweet-talked her way into their hearts. But soon the Humans envied those who played with her, hating those she embraced. And even when she hugged them, it was never enough, for they feared they were a squeeze and a hug from her hugging and squeezing someone else.

Even spring grew fickle, turning warm, then cold. Sunny, then cloudy. Some of Mother Nature's best flowers had to grow up right through the snow!

Mother Nature pulled up a mountain and began to cry. She let out a mighty wail! Her tears turned ponds into lakes, lakes into seas, and seas into oceans.

"I know exactly how you feel, ma'am," her oldest friend, West Wind, comforted. "Just human nature, that's all! My zephyrs all hanker to be breezes. Little ol' breezes want to be gales. My gales are pie-eyed after being hurricanes. My eldest sashayed himself into a regular twister. Still, try an' try again, like they say."

"Try again?" shouted Mother Nature. "What would I make a child out of?"

"You oughta thought of that before you wept everything away," West Wind chided.

"You oughta make a child more like
me. Wild and free! Kind that knows
where he's goin' and gits there." On that
parting thought, West Wind galloped
over the edge of the world.

"Oh, tush, tush!" said East Wind, polishing up a sunrise on the opposite edge. "Your child should be made of such stuff as I! Polished! Poised!"

"No, no, no!" piped North Wind. "This baby's got to

be cool! Cool, mommy-o, cool! Cool like the driven snow.

Yeah! Yeah! Like they do say!" And with that he blew till he was

all the way gone.

"My cousins surely been shootin' the breeze to you, honey!" a voice

as soft as magnolias chimed. "Seems to me what y'all need is a child the likes of

l'il ol' South Wind, me. Quiet, soft, warm, gentle. A little fresh now an' then."

South Wind blew a kiss and waltzed off.

Well, that was all good advice. So Mother Nature took a little from each, and in double time made Twins.

But when the Twins arrived, Mother Nature took one look at them and nearly went back to wailing. They were so small, one had to look twice to know they were there at all. The only one she dared let play with them was little Fear.

Fear trembled, of course. But the Twins spoke softly and gently. They didn't seem scary at all.

And they played together beautifully. And
Mother Nature watched.

When she saw how well the Twins played with
Fear, she let them play with Envy. The Twins were so
small and ordinary, he didn't seem to mind. Try as
he might, Envy couldn't find anything about them to
envy.

And they played together beautifully. And
Mother Nature watched.

Greed rushed up, grabbing the Twins away from his brothers. But he couldn't hold on.

The Twins were so giving: They gave him a good night's sleep. His shoes got new soles. They gave with all their hearts. Therefore, there was nothing left for Greed to take.

And they played together beautifully. And Mother Nature watched.

When Hate saw the fun his brothers were having, he tried to shout them down. But they kept right on playing! This made Hate angry. He tried to drown them with growls, but when the babies did not cry or cower or run, Hate became confused. They were so tiny, he couldn't see why his brothers even liked them. So he took a second look, and this time, Hate actually saw something he liked.

The Winds blew a happy laugh. They laughed and laughed, and all the children laughed. And they all began to play together beautifully.

And Mother Nature watched.

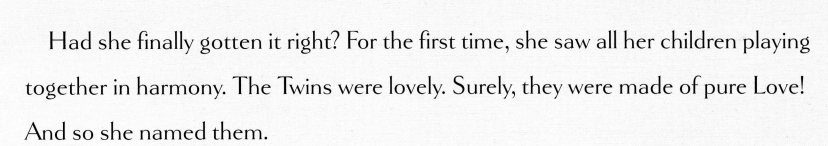

Had she finally gotten it right? For the first time, she saw all her children playing

together in harmony. The Twins were lovely. Surely, they were made of pure Love!

And so she named them.

But not all the children *always* got along. That wouldn't be human nature, now

would it?

When Fickle saw how much Love was loved, she followed their every move—

or tried to. Fickle became so loving, in fact, that down to this day,

she's often mistaken for Love. Especially by Humans.

But not by those who learn to look twice!

A Note

Whether for the young or young at heart, *Suite for Human Nature* was written to celebrate humanity, with all its shortcomings, and its most singular ability to love. Originally performed at Jazz at Lincoln Center, esteemed lyricist Diane Charlotte Lampert and Pulitzer Prize—winning trumpeter and composer Wynton Marsalis collaborated for twelve years to create this allegory about the creation of love. And now, here, Diane shares it with you—this time with stunning paintings (done on linen cloth) by Eric Puybaret, once again reminding us that while love cannot cure all, it can teach us to balance our capricious nature and can, most importantly, transform every one of us.